BALLPARK Mysteries 15

THE BALTIMORE BANDIT

Also by David A. Kelly
BALLPARK MYSTERIES®

THE MVP SERIES

Babe Ruth and the Baseball Curse

BALLPARK Mysteries 15

THE BALTIMORE BANDIT

by David A. Kelly

illustrated by Mark Meyers

A STEPPING STONE BOOK™
Random House 🏠 New York

This book is dedicated to Alison Kolani and all the other great copy editors at Random House who have saved me from countless embarrassments by finding mistakes and problems in all my Ballpark Mysteries and MVP books. The key to a good book is great editors. Thank you!
—D.A.K.

"You could be a kid for as long as you want when you play baseball."
—Cal Ripken Jr., Baltimore Orioles shortstop and third baseman, 1981–2001

Text copyright © 2019 by David A. Kelly
Cover art and interior illustrations copyright © 2019 by Mark Meyers

All rights reserved. Published in the United States by Random House Children's Books, a division of Penguin Random House LLC, New York.

Random House and the colophon are registered trademarks and A Stepping Stone Book and the colophon are trademarks of Penguin Random House LLC. Ballpark Mysteries® is a registered trademark of Upside Research, Inc.

Visit us on the Web!
rhcbooks.com

Educators and librarians, for a variety of teaching tools, visit us at
RHTeachersLibrarians.com

Library of Congress Cataloging-in-Publication Data
Names: Kelly, David A., author. | Meyers, Mark, illustrator.
Title: The Baltimore bandit / by David A. Kelly ; illustrated by Mark Meyers.
Description: First edition. | New York: Random House, 2019. | Series: Ballpark mysteries ; 15 | "A Stepping Stone book." | Summary: Babe Ruth's baseball glove goes missing before a Baltimore Orioles game. It's up to cousins Mike and Kate to find its whereabouts."—Provided by publisher.
Identifiers: LCCN 2018010433 | ISBN 978-1-5247-6754-9 (trade) |
ISBN 978-1-5247-6755-6 (lib. bdg.) | ISBN 978-1-5247-6756-3 (ebook)
Subjects: | CYAC: Baltimore Orioles (Baseball team)—Fiction. | Baseball—Fiction. | Cousins—Fiction. | Stealing—Fiction. | Baltimore (Md.)—Fiction.
Classification: LCC PZ7.K2936 Ban 2019 | DDC [Fic]—dc23

Printed in the United States of America
10 9 8 7 6 5 4 3 2 1

This book has been officially leveled by using the F&P Text Level Gradient™ Leveling System.

Random House Children's Books supports the First Amendment
and celebrates the right to read.

Contents

A Golden Slide

"POW!" Mike Walsh said as he swung an imaginary bat. "Babe Ruth blasts a home run in Baltimore!"

Mike's cousin Kate Hopkins watched his pretend baseball fly over the Orioles' outfield. "UH-OH! CRASH!" she said in an announcer's voice. "He's the first player to hit a window on the big brick warehouse across the street!"

It was late on a Sunday afternoon, and Mike and Kate were waiting in line to run the bases after a Baltimore Orioles game.

"Well then, maybe *I* hit it!" Mike said.

"And if *you* hit it, you'll have to pay for the broken window!" Kate said.

Mike shrugged. "Okay, I guess I'll let Babe Ruth take that one," he said. "But he can't have pancakes with Flaps!"

Mike and Kate had come to Baltimore with Kate's mom, Laura Hopkins. She was a sports reporter for American Sportz. She had arranged for Mike and Kate to meet the Orioles star pitcher Flaps Palmer the following day for a pregame meal. Flaps was superstitious. Before each game he pitched, he insisted on having flapjacks for good luck.

"I might not be able to hit as well as Babe Ruth," Mike said. "But I'll bet I can keep up with Flaps when it comes to eating pancakes!"

Kate nodded. "When it comes to pancakes, you could keep up with a vacuum cleaner!"

Mike smiled. "Yes, but I'd enjoy them more than the vacuum would!"

Mrs. Hopkins and the kids had arrived earlier that day from their home in Cooperstown, New York. They had watched the Sunday-afternoon Orioles game at Oriole Park at Camden Yards. They also had front-row seats near the dugout for the next day's game against the Seattle Mariners.

Mike pointed to a long, eight-story brick warehouse behind the Orioles' outfield. "Actually, I don't think Babe Ruth could have hit one of the windows in that warehouse," he said.

"Why not?" Kate asked.

"Because back then, the Orioles played in a different stadium," Mike said. "Also, even though he was born right near here, Babe Ruth was traded from the Orioles to the Boston Red

Sox halfway through his first season. Back then, he was a pitcher, just like Flaps."

"I'll bet that's why Flaps is crazy about Babe Ruth," Kate said. "At the ceremony before the game, they said Flaps is a huge fan!"

During the ceremony, a valuable baseball glove that Babe Ruth once owned had been unveiled. It was an old, flat, brown glove, but it was worth over $250,000! The Orioles were going to put it on display in a room near the gift shop for the first time before the next day's game.

"Hey, look—it's our turn!" Kate said. "We're going to run the bases at a major-league stadium!"

"I know!" Mike said. "This is awesome!" He high-fived Kate.

A man standing in front of the Orioles' dugout motioned for Mike and Kate to head to the batter's box. He wore a black-and-orange

Orioles jersey and had a big bushy beard. On his baseball cap was an image of a large white crab.

Before Mike and Kate reached home plate, they heard the first few bars of "Take Me Out to the Ball Game." The man held up his hand to motion for Mike and Kate to stop. Then he reached into his pocket and pulled out his phone, which played the song as its ringtone.

The man answered the phone. While he talked, Mike pulled a tennis ball out of the pocket in his shorts and tossed it to Kate. They played catch until the man hung up. He waved at Mike and Kate and pointed at home plate. Mike slipped the ball back into his pocket, and they ran over.

"Ready to run the bases like a Baltimore Oriole?" he asked. "Are you two doing this together?"

Kate nodded.

"Stand in the batter's box," he said. "Take off when I say 'Go!'"

Kate and Mike crouched down, ready to run.

"Five, four, three, two, one . . . GO!" the man shouted.

Mike and Kate took off like a shot. Kate seized an early lead as she and Mike raced for first base.

"Mike Walsh has ripped another line drive deep to center field," Mike called as he ran. "It's another amazing hit by this young superstar."

Kate's foot touched first base just before Mike's. They headed to second.

"Mike Walsh is tearing up the base paths today!" Mike yelled. He pulled a step ahead of Kate.

A small cloud of dust rose behind them as they rounded second. Kate seemed to find extra power and shot ahead again, but Mike caught up near third. They thundered down on third base and headed for home.

"It looks like it will be close!" Mike called out. "Will Mike Walsh beat the throw? I think he will!"

Kate zoomed toward home plate. She was a step ahead of Mike.

Mike made a split-second decision to slide. His heel hit the white rubber edge of home plate just as Kate's right foot landed squarely in the center of the plate.

"Home run!" she cried. "I win!"

Mike slid across home plate, leaving a trail of dust behind him.

"No way!" Mike said as he stood up. "My foot touched first. *I* won!"

"No, *I* won!" Kate said.

"Let's ask your mom," Mike said. Mrs. Hopkins had been standing just behind home plate, watching them. "Who won, Aunt Laura?"

"It was very close," Mrs. Hopkins said. "It's possible that Kate's foot landed first. You *were* behind her, Mike."

Mike held up his hands. "I know!" he said. "That's why I was sliding!"

Mike pointed to the far side of the plate. "I started sliding right over there, and my foot crossed . . . ," he said.

Kate and Mrs. Hopkins waited for Mike to finish his thought, but he didn't. Instead, he scuffed at the dirt in the batter's box with the tip of his sneaker.

"Mike? Is something wrong?" Mrs. Hopkins asked.

Mike ignored them. He dropped to the ground, dug with his fingers, and then tugged something from the dirt.

Sunlight sparkled off a shiny gold coin.

"Look what I found," Mike said. "Buried treasure!"

A Birdman in
Birdland

"Buried treasure?" Kate asked. "In Camden Yards?"

Kate ran over to Mike and studied the gold coin. It was a little bit bigger than a quarter, and it had a picture of Babe Ruth on the front and the words *Babe Ruth #1* on the back. "Why would someone bury treasure under home plate?" she asked.

Mike smiled. He took

the coin back from Kate and slipped it into his pocket. "I don't know," he said. "Maybe it's my reward for winning the race!"

"I don't know about that," Kate said. "I'm not even sure you won the race!"

Mike sighed. "We can have a do-over at home," he said. "It would be fun to keep the coin, but I should probably turn it in to the Orioles. Maybe I'll get a big reward!"

"That's a great idea, Mike," Mrs. Hopkins said. "You can turn it in tomorrow at the lost-and-found office before your pancakes with Flaps!"

Mike knocked on the door labeled LOST AND FOUND. It was just after noon the next day. The office was in the big brick warehouse behind the Orioles' outfield. The game was going to start in a little over an hour, and the stadium was starting to fill with fans. Mrs. Hopkins had gone up to the pressroom to work.

Kate peeked through the window in the door. "I don't think anyone is there yet," she said. "It doesn't even look like there's a light on."

Mike slipped the coin back into his pocket. "Well, I guess I get to keep it for a little while longer," he said. "I sure hope there's a reward for finding real gold coins!"

"Real gold! Real gold!" a voice squawked from behind them.

Mike and Kate spun around. Standing behind them was a man with an orange-and-black bird on his shoulder! The man was wearing an Orioles jersey and baseball cap.

"Real gold!" the bird squawked again.

Kate leaned forward to get a better look at

the bird and the man. "Hey, orioles can't talk!" she said.

The bird bobbed its head. "Stolen base!" it squawked. "Stolen base!"

"Orioles are black and orange," Kate said. "But that's not an oriole! That's a parrot dressed as an oriole!"

The bird's bright green feathers were mostly hidden by a bird-size black-and-orange sweater.

The man tipped his cap back and squinted at Kate with one eye closed. He shook his head. "This is not a parrot," he said. "It's Edgar. Edgar's an oriole!"

Kate watched the bird. It stepped back and forth on the man's shoulder and tilted its head as it looked down at Mike and Kate.

"Aw! Double play! Double play!" the bird

squawked. Then it whistled the opening notes to "Take Me Out to the Ball Game."

"Hey, that's new," the man said. "He's always picking up new tricks! He's one smart oriole."

Kate shook her head. "That's no oriole," she said again. "Orioles can't talk!"

"Edgar can," the man said. "You just heard him talk!"

"I know I heard him talk," Kate said. "But

that doesn't mean he's an oriole. Edgar's a parrot. *They* can talk."

The man shifted his weight to his other foot. He glanced at Edgar. He gave a shrug. "Well, maybe . . . ," he mumbled. "It doesn't really matter what he is, as long as he's an Orioles fan!"

"So are we!" Mike said. "That's Kate, and I'm Mike. I know they call this stadium Birdland, so I guess we shouldn't be surprised to find real birds here!"

The man held out his hand. "And I'm the Birdman," he said. "My real name is Clinton Kelly. But everyone around here calls me Birdman because I bring Edgar to the games. He loves baseball, and he's a fast learner. We have a stand down in the Kids' Corner area of the ballpark. If you stop by during the game, you can have your picture taken with him for free!"

"Cool!" Kate said.

The man pointed at the door. "The lost and found doesn't open until later," he said. "Can I help you? Did you say you found something made of gold?"

Mike nodded. "I found a gold coin down on the field," he said. "I'm hoping there's a big reward for it."

The man lifted an eyebrow and looked around. "Why don't you give me the coin? I can turn it in for you when they open."

The Birdman held out his hand.

"Real gold!" Edgar squawked.

"That's okay," Mike said. He nudged Kate to move along. "Thanks for the offer, Birdman. But we're late for pancakes!"

The Birdman waved to them. "No problem," he said. "See you at the Kids' Corner!"

Hot Flapjacks

"What was up with him?" Kate asked. She and Mike had just turned the corner and were heading to meet Flaps for pancakes.

Mike reached into his pocket and pulled out the gold coin. "I don't know," he said. "There's no way I'm giving this to anyone but the lost-and-found people."

They wound their way through the stadium to the lower level near the Orioles' clubhouse. After a security guard checked for their names on a clipboard, he waved them past. "Head down that hallway," he said. "Flaps will be in the second room on the left."

Mike and Kate ran down the hallway. As soon as they entered the room, they could smell cinnamon and apples.

"Hey, you're just in time," said a tall, blond baseball player in full uniform. It was Flaps. "I'm glad your mom set this up. It's fun to have fans like you join me for some flapjacks!"

Flaps was standing in front of a long table piled with pancakes, orange juice, and bacon. He lifted his head a little and sniffed. "Smells great, right?" he said. "I asked for apple-cinnamon flapjacks today!"

"We heard you really like flapjacks," Mike said.

"Like them? I love them!" Flaps said. "Pancakes, wheat cakes, batter cakes, griddle

cakes, johnnycakes, hotcakes, slapjacks, and flapjacks. Whatever you call them, I'll eat them! And you should, too! Let's dig in. They make them specially for me and anyone else on the team who wants them."

Flaps motioned for Mike and Kate to take a seat at a table. A few of his teammates sat nearby. Flaps plunked down his long frame and drizzled maple syrup all over a tall pile of pancakes. He quickly took a forkful and wolfed it down.

"*¡Guau, tantos panqueques!*" Kate said. "That's a lot of pancakes!" She was teaching herself Spanish. She liked to practice it whenever she had a chance.

"It sure is!" Flaps said with a grin.

As Kate and Mike filled their plates with pancakes and tried to keep up, Flaps pointed his fork at them.

"There's only one thing I like more than flapjacks," Flaps said. "And that's Babe Ruth! He was a great hitter. But most people don't know he started out as a great pitcher. I've always wanted to be as good a pitcher as the Babe."

"And I always wanted to be as good a batter as the Babe," Mike said.

"Just not in that charity baseball game in 1931 when a girl named Jackie Mitchell struck

Ruth out," Kate said. "And she was only seventeen years old! I'd like to be Jackie Mitchell!"

Mike rolled his eyes. "Well, you can't hit home runs without striking out sometimes," he said. "I'd still give anything to be like Babe Ruth. He set a record by hitting seven hundred fourteen home runs!" Mike looked at Flaps, who smiled. "That reminds me," Mike said. He dug around in his pocket as Flaps took another bite of pancakes.

"If you like Babe Ruth, you'll like this," Mike said. He pulled the coin out of his pocket and put it on the table.

Flaps's eyes grew wide and a smile crossed his face. "Hey, where did you get that?" he asked.

"The batter's box!" Mike said. "I slid into home plate yesterday and found it in the dirt."

Flaps reached into his pocket and pulled

something out. He held his hand a few inches above the table and slowly opened it.

Clink! Clink! Clink! Clink! Clink! Clink!

Flaps dumped about twenty coins on the table!

Mike and Kate leaned forward and looked at the pile of gold. Mike dropped the slice of bacon he was eating.

"This must be worth a thousand dollars!" Mike said as he reached out and ran his fingers through the pile of coins.

Flaps laughed. "I'm afraid not," he said. "These aren't real gold. They're only worth about a quarter each."

Kate picked up a handful and let them slip through her fingers back to the table. "Why do you have so many?" she asked.

Flaps held up a coin in his right hand. "I give them out when someone wants my signature,"

he said. "I don't sign autographs, because it would strain my pitching hand."

Mike pointed to his coin. "But why was this one buried in the batter's box?" he asked.

Flaps looked over each of his shoulders and then leaned forward. "Can you keep a secret?" he asked.

Mike and Kate leaned closer. "Yes!" they both said at once. "We're detectives—we're good at keeping secrets."

"I put it there!" Flaps said with a big smile.

"But why?" Kate asked.

"For good luck!" Flaps said. "I thought maybe I'd be able to strike out batters like Babe did if I put a lucky coin in the ground under the batters' feet."

"Too bad you can't put a trapdoor under the batter and press a button when the count gets to three balls," Kate said. "Once the batter dropped into the ground, you could strike him out without worrying!"

Mike and Flaps laughed. Then Flaps shook his head. "Now that's a good idea," he said, "but I don't think the commissioner of baseball would allow trapdoors under the batter's box. That reminds me of the other reason I buried the coin in the field. Have you heard about what they found under second base?"

"No! What?" Mike and Kate asked.

"Babe Ruth's house!" Flaps said. "Babe Ruth's father used to own a tavern right near the B&O Railroad warehouse that's on Eutaw Street behind the outfield. His family lived above it. When they were building the Orioles ballpark, they dug up parts of the house where

Babe Ruth had once lived. It was right between second base and center field."

"Wow!" Kate said. "You sure know a lot about Babe Ruth."

Flaps nodded as he lifted a big forkful of pancakes to his mouth. "I sure do," he said. "I can't wait to see Babe Ruth's glove when they put it on display tomorrow. I'd give *anything* to own something like that."

Mike, Kate, and Flaps continued to munch on pancakes and drink orange juice for the next fifteen minutes. As they ate, Flaps told other stories about Babe Ruth and the Baltimore Orioles.

Just as they finished eating, a woman in an Orioles jacket ran into the room.

"Flaps! Flaps!" the woman said. "You'll never believe what just happened!"

Flaps looked up. "This is my friend Sandra," he said to Mike and Kate. Flaps tipped his hat. "What are you so worked up about, Sandy?" he asked.

"There are Babe Ruth bandits in Birdland!" Sandra said. "Babe Ruth's baseball glove has been stolen! I overheard the police talking to the gift shop manager."

"Oh no!" Flaps said. "That's terrible!"

Sandra nodded. "I know," she said. "But that's not the worst part."

"What do you mean?" Kate asked. "What could be worse than Babe Ruth's glove being stolen?"

Sandra turned to Mike and Kate. "The police think Flaps stole it!"

A Flappy Clue?

"Me?" Flaps said. "Why would I steal it?"

Sandra walked over to the table. "People know how much you love Babe Ruth," she said. "I guess you're a natural suspect."

Flaps pointed at Mike. "But *everyone* loves Babe Ruth," he said. "Even Mike here is a huge Babe Ruth fan. I don't know why they'd suspect me."

Sandra leaned over and picked up one of Flaps's Babe Ruth coins. It clinked as she dropped it back into the pile. "Maybe because when they were investigating, they found one of these *inside* the safe where the glove was," she said.

"What?" Flaps said. "How can that be?"

Sandra nodded. "And no glove!" she added. "You'd better go talk with the security team before the game. They're over at the stockroom

in the gift shop. The manager was storing Babe's glove in the safe there."

Flaps pushed his chair back and stood up. He shook his head as he started to walk to the door. "I don't have much time! I have to pitch soon!" he said. "If we lose this game, we won't be in first place and may not make the playoffs!"

Sandra followed Flaps out.

Mike glanced at Kate, and then nodded at the huge stacks of pancakes on the table. "Well, I've lost my appetite," he said.

"Me too, at least for pancakes," she said. "But not for catching the Babe Ruth bandit! We need to find that glove!"

Mike ran his fingers through the gold coins that Flaps had left on the table, and then put his coin back in his pocket. "It's worth lots of money," he said. "But I can't believe that Flaps would have taken it."

"I can't, either," Kate said. "He seems awfully nice." She stood. "I think we need to investigate. Let's go check the gift shop."

Mike jumped up from the table. He and Kate ran through the stadium, past fans finding their seats and long lines of people at food stands. In the background, an announcer's voice boomed over the loudspeakers.

A few minutes later, Mike and Kate were on the other side of the stadium. They were standing in front of the long brick warehouse that was once used by the B&O Railroad. To their left was the Orioles' gift shop. On their right was a fancy restaurant. In between was a small area with a sign overhead labeled BABE RUTH AND BALTIMORE.

"Sandra said the glove was stolen from the gift shop's stockroom," Kate said. "Let's see if we can find it."

Kate and Mike entered the gift shop. They pretended to look at all the different hats, T-shirts, jerseys, and Oriole-themed gifts while searching for the stockroom door.

"There it is," Mike said. He pointed to the back corner. "Just keep browsing and we'll head that way."

Right next to the stockroom door was a large counter of Orioles jackets. The door was open slightly, and as they passed, Mike and Kate peeked in and spotted Flaps talking to two security guards. Mike tugged Kate's shirt and ducked behind the counter to listen.

"How could you think I took the glove?" Flaps asked.

"We're not saying you did it," one security

guard said. "It's just that the police found one of your gold coins inside the safe where the glove had been. They had to list you as a suspect."

"But I was eating pancakes!" Flaps said. "When was the glove stolen?"

"We put the glove in that safe this morning at ten o'clock," the second security guard said. "The museum director was coming by around lunch today to install it in the Babe Ruth and Baltimore exhibit next door. But when she opened the safe at noon, the glove was gone."

"What were you doing this morning between ten o'clock and twelve o'clock?" the first guard asked Flaps.

"I was running errands," Flaps said.

"Was anyone with you?" the second guard asked.

"Um, no," Flaps said. "I was alone."

"Well, we can check into that later," the first guard said. "The police just left. They dusted for fingerprints and took pictures of the crime scene. We'll let you know if we hear anything from them or have further questions for you."

"But I didn't take it!" Flaps said. "Didn't you find any other clues in here? I can't be the only suspect!"

"No, we didn't find any other clues," the second guard said. "As far as we know, the only people who have access to this room are people who work here, or people who are in the stadium. At this point, I'm afraid everyone is a suspect, including you."

Flaps sighed. "I can't believe this is happening," he said. "I've got a game to win. You can find me afterward if you have more questions, okay?"

"Yes," the first security guard said. "We'll be in touch."

Flaps's cleats clattered as he headed for the door of the gift shop.

Mike and Kate pushed themselves in between the jackets as Flaps hurried by. A few moments later, one of the security guards' walkie-talkies crackled with a call from the main office. The guard spoke with her supervisor and then slipped the radio onto a holder on her belt.

"The game's starting. We should head back to the office," she said to the other guard. "We've got to wait to hear from the police before we do anything else."

"Give me a minute to finish my notes," the other guard said.

When the guards left the stockroom, Mike popped his head up to watch them make their way out of the gift shop. Then he pulled the gold coin out of his pocket and showed it to Kate.

"Come on," he said. "I've got an idea!"

They stepped out of the rack of jackets. Mike walked over to the stockroom door. He flipped the coin in the air a few times and then let it drop. It clinked on the floor and rolled away.

"Oops!" he said to Kate with a smile. "My coin just rolled into the stockroom. Can you come help me find it?"

They quietly opened the door and slipped through it. On the way in, Mike picked his coin up. Inside the room, metal shelves with cardboard boxes of goods lined the walls. In the far corner stood an empty wooden table. In another corner, on the floor, was a metal safe. Its door was open.

Mike and Kate crossed the room and knelt

in front of the safe, but there wasn't much to see. It was empty.

"Whoever broke in must have known how to open the safe," Kate said. "Let's check the rest of the room."

They studied the brown cardboard boxes on the metal shelves and looked under the empty wooden table. But they didn't find anything helpful.

After a few minutes of searching for clues, Kate turned to Mike. "I don't see anything," she said.

"I don't, either," Mike said.

Mike knelt to look at the safe one more time. It was still empty. He studied its edge to see if anyone had forced it open, but there were no pry marks on it. He was just about to get up when a glint of color caught his eye from the dark, narrow space beneath the safe.

Mike dropped down on his stomach. "Hang on!" he said.

Mike poked his fingers under the safe and wiggled them around. A moment later, he grabbed hold of an object and sprang up from the floor. Something green shimmered in his hand.

"Look," he said. "I found a clue!"

Captured!

"A feather!" Kate said. She took it from Mike to get a closer look. It was bright green and about the length of Mike's hand. "The Birdman!"

"That's what I was thinking!" Mike said. "This must be one of Edgar's feathers! The glove was taken this morning before lunch. And we know that the Birdman was here today. He could have come over with Edgar and stolen the glove."

"Let's go find the Birdman," Kate said. She

slipped the feather into her pocket and headed for the door.

Mike quietly closed the stockroom door behind them, and they crept out of the gift shop.

By this time, the stadium was filled with people rooting for the Orioles. As Mike and Kate passed the patio overlooking the outfield, they heard a big cheer from the crowd.

"Hang on!" Mike said. "I want to see how Flaps is doing." Kate followed him over to the Flag Court patio. It was a large open deck filled with flags from all the other American League teams.

Flaps wasn't doing well. Even though the score was still 0–0, the Orioles were in trouble. It was only the first inning, and Flaps had loaded the bases!

"Oh no!" Kate said. "He's struggling!"

Mike and Kate watched as Flaps pitched.

The first two pitches were high and outside. The third pitch bounced in the dirt. The catcher had to work hard to stop it. Three balls! The batter didn't swing at any.

With the count at three balls and no strikes, Flaps threw another pitch. This one was right over the plate. The batter swung with all his might, making contact with a loud *CRACK*. The ball flew high over the shortstop's head.

"Yikes!" Mike cried.

The Seattle Mariners runners took off. The man on third base crossed home plate. Then the player from second base scored! Finally, the Orioles centerfielder threw the ball to the cutoff man, who threw it to the catcher. The runners stopped. Flaps had let up a double. The score was now 2–0, Seattle.

The Orioles fans went quiet. It didn't look like a good day for Flaps or the Orioles.

Kate tugged on Mike's T-shirt. "Come on," she said. "We've got to find that glove!"

Mike and Kate dodged fans as they ran for the Kids' Corner, near right field. As they left the Flag Court patio, Mike pointed to a food stand and sniffed the air. "Mmm . . . ," he said. "Barbecue! Let's come back after we find the glove!"

"Okay!" Kate agreed.

They continued on and passed a giant black-and-orange statue of an oriole with a bat. Around the corner was a large space filled with activities for kids.

"Oh, cool!" Mike said. "A bouncy house, Skee-Ball, and a climbing structure with slides! And the baseball game behind us! We've got everything we need right here."

"But all we really need is the Birdman," Kate said. "And there he is!"

Kate pointed to the far corner of the space. The Birdman was standing in front of a large picture of the Orioles' stadium. Edgar the parrot sat on the shoulder of a little girl next to him. Mike and Kate watched as the Birdman took pictures of the girl with Edgar.

When the girl finished, Mike and Kate walked over. "Keep an eye out for the stolen glove," Mike whispered. "Or anything big enough to be a hiding place for the glove."

"Oh, hello again!" the Birdman said when he noticed Mike and Kate. "Did you want to have your photo taken with Edgar? Or were you going to let me help you with that gold coin?"

"Real gold! Real gold!" Edgar squawked. His head bobbed back and forth as he looked from Mike to Kate.

"Turns out the coin wasn't real gold after all," Mike said. He shrugged. "But it's still neat."

"Oh, that's too bad," the Birdman said.

"Yes," Kate said. "But we would love to get a picture with Edgar. And we have a couple of questions for you, too."

"Sure," the Birdman said. "Stand here." He motioned for Mike and Kate to come over in front of the ballpark background. He placed Edgar on Kate's shoulder.

"Play ball! Play ball!" Edgar screeched. Then he started whistling "Take Me Out to the Ball Game" again.

Mike nodded his head in time to Edgar's whistling. "Buy me some peanuts and Cracker Jack, I don't care if I *never* get back!" Mike sang. "Good job, Edgar! How did you know I was hungry?"

"Because you're always hungry, Mike!" Kate said.

The Birdman laughed. "Edgar just picked

up that song today," he said. "I don't know where he learned it, but I can't believe that I never thought of teaching it to him before! It's perfect!"

Kate giggled as Edgar danced back and forth on her shoulder. "Come on, let's take a picture!" she said. Kate leaned forward slowly and handed the Birdman her phone. He stood back and snapped some photos. In between shots, Mike and Kate scanned the Birdman's area for the glove or something big enough to put the glove in. But they didn't see anything. The Birdman moved Edgar to Mike's shoulder and took a few more shots.

"I think that's good," the Birdman said. He walked over and took Edgar back from Mike's shoulder. "Now, what did you need to ask me?"

"It's about Flaps," Mike said.

"Oh yes, I know," the Birdman said. "He's not doing well today!"

"No, that's the thing," Kate said. "We think he has other things on his mind. Like the Babe Ruth glove they unveiled yesterday. It was stolen!"

Just then, Edgar started whistling again. At first it sounded like a police whistle. But it was "Take Me Out to the Ball Game" again.

"Edgar! Shhh! I'm having a conversation," the Birdman said. "Yes, I heard about that. It's too bad. I hope they find that glove!"

"We do, too," Mike said. "That's why we're here."

"What do you mean?" the Birdman asked.

"Because," Kate said, "we think *you* stole Babe Ruth's glove!"

Hello? We Have a Clue!

"What?" the Birdman asked. "Is this a joke?"

"No," Kate said. "And it's no joke that the police think that Flaps stole the glove."

"But I've got nothing to do with it!" the Birdman said. "Why do you think I stole it?"

Kate stepped forward. "Easy," she said. She held up the green feather and held it next to Edgar. "We found this feather under the safe in the stockroom. The safe that *used* to hold Babe Ruth's glove. Look! It's a perfect match!"

The Birdman stared at the feather. "You're right," he said with a nod.

"Then you did it!" Mike said. "The feather proves that you were in the gift shop's stockroom this morning with Edgar!"

The Birdman took a step back. "Well, you're right again," he said.

Mike glanced at Kate and smiled. "I *knew* he took Babe Ruth's glove!" he said.

The Birdman held up his hands. "No, I didn't," he said.

"What do you mean?" Kate asked.

The Birdman smiled. "I *was* in the stockroom this morning with Edgar," he said. "But I *didn't* take Babe Ruth's glove."

The Birdman lifted Edgar off his shoulder and placed him in a tall metal cage nearby. Then he turned back to Mike and Kate.

"You found the feather because I put Edgar

in the gift shop's stockroom while I get ready before each game," he said. "I left him there for a couple of hours, starting at ten o'clock this morning. I put his cage on the wooden table in the corner of the stockroom, like I always do. He loses a few feathers every now and then. One of them probably just blew under the safe."

"That doesn't prove that you didn't take the glove," Kate said. "You *were* in the room."

The Birdman laughed. "You're very persistent," he said. "But that doesn't mean you're right! I wasn't alone in the stockroom. My friend Ernie was with me the whole time." The Birdman waved to the man running the bouncy house. "Hey, Ernie! These kids want to know if you were with me this morning in the stockroom."

Ernie nodded and called back, "Yup! I was with him the whole time, like always. We usually help each other get set up. And I help him carry Edgar."

"Thanks," the Birdman said. He turned to Mike and Kate. "I didn't take the Babe Ruth glove, and I don't know who did. Sorry!"

"We're glad it wasn't you. Sorry we thought it might be," Mike said. "We'll just have to keep looking!"

"I've got to get back to my customers," the Birdman said. "Let me know if there's anything I can do to help!" He turned to a family who was waiting to meet Edgar.

Kate looked at Mike. "Do you believe him?" she asked.

Mike shrugged. "I don't know," he said. "It seems like he and Ernie are telling us the truth. But maybe they're working together and they're good liars. We need to keep digging."

Kate nodded. "I agree," she said. "Let's head

to our seats to see how Flaps is doing. We can figure out what to do next from there."

Mike and Kate made their way to their seats near the Orioles' dugout. Mike pointed to the scoreboard. "Oh no, look at the score!" he said. The Orioles were losing by four! A Seattle player was up at bat, and Flaps was still pitching.

"Come on, Flaps!" he cried. "You can do it!"

Flaps wound up and pitched. The ball sailed high and outside. The batter tossed his bat gently to the side and jogged to first base. "The Orioles aren't going to win by walking the batters," Mike said.

Flaps was able to get the next batter out, so all hope wasn't lost for the Orioles. The following batter worked Flaps to three balls and two strikes and then hit a single. The man on first advanced to second. Flaps needed an out.

The fans stood up and cheered for the

Orioles. "Come on, Flaps!" Kate called. "Strike him out!" She and Mike clapped and yelled.

Flaps studied the batter and then threw a fastball down the middle of the plate. The batter swung. Strike one!

Mike and Kate cheered more!

Flaps waited for the sign from the catcher and prepared to throw again. This time, he threw a curveball. But the batter swung and got a piece of it! The ball sailed in between the first baseman and the shortstop for a double.

"I don't think the pancakes are helping him today," Mike said.

The catcher walked out to talk to Flaps on the mound. Flaps put his glove in front of his mouth so the other team couldn't tell what he was saying.

Mike nudged Kate's knee. He pointed to the big scoreboard in the outfield. It had a clock in the middle and two metal orioles on either side. "Those birds are weather vanes," he said. "They're supposed to tell the batters which way the wind is blowing. But the players say they don't work. Instead, if you want to know which way the wind is blowing, look at the smoke from the barbecue stand behind the scoreboard!"

"That's funny," Kate said. "I guess you just need to know what to look for."

Mike nodded. "And maybe it's the same with Babe Ruth's glove," he said. "Maybe we're not looking for the right thing."

"What do you mean?" Kate asked.

"The Birdman didn't steal the glove like we thought," Mike said. "But we know he was in the stockroom right around the time the glove was stolen. What if he saw a clue or heard something strange when he was doing it? We forgot to ask him if he spotted anything unusual today!"

Don't Be Crabby!

"You're right!" Kate said. She stood up and started to head for the walkway. "It's worth a try."

Mike and Kate ran back through the stadium to the Kids' Corner. The Birdman had just finished taking pictures of a little boy with Edgar when they arrived.

"Birdman?" Mike asked. "We had one more question for you. When you dropped off and

picked up Edgar, did you happen to see anything or anyone unusual?"

The Birdman leaned back and thought for
a little bit. "Hmmm," he said. "I said hello to
Judy the cashier at the gift shop when Ernie
and I walked in. But we didn't see anything
strange near the stockroom."

"Okay, thanks anyway," Mike said. He
turned to Kate. "We should go talk to Judy, in
case she saw something."

"And Ernie, too," Kate added.

"Foul ball!" Edgar squawked.

Mike leaned over to Edgar. "I know you can
talk, but I wish you could answer questions!"
he said. "You must know who stole the glove
because you were in the room when it happened! How about a little clue?"

The Birdman laughed. "I'm afraid Edgar

can only repeat what he's learned," he said. "If he could have a real conversation, I'd be a millionaire!"

Kate laughed.

"Come on, Edgar! Did you see someone strange in the stockroom?" Mike asked. "Who broke into the safe?" He waited for an answer from Edgar, but the bird just glanced from Mike to the Birdman.

Mike shrugged. "I guess he didn't see anyone," he said. "Maybe he was sleeping. Or maybe he doesn't want to talk!"

As Mike turned to walk back to Kate, Edgar gave a shrill whistle. Then he launched into "Take Me Out to the Ball Game" again.

Mike started bobbing his head and humming along. "Edgar's telling us we need to head back to the ball game since we're out of ideas," he said. He hummed a few more seconds and then stopped. "Or maybe he's giving us what I asked for. A clue!"

The Birdman stared at Mike. "What do you mean?" he asked. "How can Edgar be telling you a clue? What did he say?"

"It's not what he said," Mike said. "It's what he whistled."

Mike licked his lips and puckered up. As Kate and the Birdman listened, he whistled

"Take Me Out to the Ball Game." "Edgar's been whistling that all day," he said. "You even said that today was the first time you had ever heard Edgar whistle that song!"

"That's right," the Birdman said. "I don't know where he picked it up."

"I do," Mike said. "Because Kate and I have heard that song before. In fact, we heard it here yesterday."

Kate nodded. "After the game," she said. "When we were running the bases. The man who told us when to start had a phone that played 'Take Me Out to the Ball Game'!"

"Bingo!" Mike said. "What if he's the thief and his phone rang while he was in the stockroom stealing the glove? His phone would have played 'Take Me Out to the Ball Game'! That's how Edgar learned it. And he kept whistling it to tell us who the thief was!"

"I always knew Edgar was a smart bird," the Birdman said.

"Now we just have to find the man with the phone," Kate said. "But the Orioles don't let kids run the bases again until next Sunday."

"Do you know where he might be?" Mike asked the Birdman. "He had a big bushy beard. Any idea who he is?"

The Birdman thought for a moment. "You know, I'm not sure I do," he said. "I've seen a man at one of the food stands with a big bushy beard, but I can't remember which stand, and I'm not even sure it's the same guy."

"Okay, thanks," Kate said. "Mike and I will start by checking out the food stands."

The Birdman glanced over at the line that was forming for him and Edgar. "Good luck!" he said. "I have to get back to work."

Mike and Kate ran to the main walkway

63

around the stadium. Food stands stretched as far as they could see, interrupted only by souvenir shops and bathrooms.

"We'll have to work fast," Kate said.

"Normally, I'd love to stop at each food area," Mike said. "But today I'd rather just go to one—the one where that guy works!"

They went from one food stand to another, stepping up to the counters and checking out the workers.

"This is going to take a while," Mike said after they had stopped at their fourth food area. It was selling Mexican food. "I never realized how many food stands there are at a ballpark!"

Kate nodded. She watched as workers quickly made tacos and burritos for hungry fans. They all wore uniforms and baseball hats.

Kate grabbed Mike's arm and pointed to the

man behind the counter. "Hey, look at his hat!" she said.

The man's hat had a green and a red chili pepper on it.

"This is a Mexican food stand and all the workers have hats with chili peppers on them," Kate said. "When I saw that, it reminded me of the bushy-bearded man's hat from yesterday. It had a big crab on it! He must work at a crab

stand, so we don't need to check *all* the food stands, just ones that sell crabs!"

"Good work," Mike said. He gave Kate a high five. "Let's go!"

Mike and Kate followed the walkway around the stadium, stopping to check out each food stand.

"Look," Mike said, pointing to a gourmet hot dog stand. "Crab mac-and-cheese hot dogs!" He and Kate ran over to get a closer look at the workers behind the counter. But they were all wearing baseball hats with hot dogs on them.

"This isn't the place," Kate said.

"Nope," Mike agreed. He pointed to a potato chip stand across the walkway. "What about that place?"

He and Kate ran over and studied the menu board. "Crab chippers. What are they?" Kate asked the server.

"Delicious!" the server said with a smile. Her baseball cap had a brown potato on it. "It's a big pile of freshly made potato chips covered with cheese and crab meat! Want to try some?"

Mike took a step back. "Oh, no thanks," he said. "Maybe later!" He tugged Kate's shirt and started to walk away from the stand.

Kate reached over to feel Mike's forehead. "Are you feeling okay?" she asked. "I'm not sure I've seen you turn down free food before!"

"We've got a job to do!" he said. "No time for food right now."

As Mike and Kate reached the next food stand, Kate noticed it was the first one they had stopped at. "We've gone in a big circle!" she said. "That means the crab man must be on the upper level!"

"I know we need to find the glove, but I'm

tired of crabs!" Mike said. "Crab cakes, crab rolls, crab mac-and-cheese, crab hot dogs, crab pretzels, crab dip waffle fries, crab chippers! Crab and more crab! It's enough to make *me* crabby!"

"You don't need any foods to do that, Mike," Kate joked. "You're always crabby! Quick, let's take the escalators to the upper deck."

On the next level, they passed by food stands staffed by people wearing baseball hats with images of potatoes, hot dogs, chili peppers, ice cream cones, and more. But no crab hats.

As they were nearing the end of the upper deck, a huge cheer sounded from the crowd in the stadium.

Mike stopped. He pointed to one of the hallways leading to the seating area. "Hang on," he said. "I want to see what happened. Maybe Flaps is doing better!"

"Okay," Kate said.

As Mike turned to walk down the hallway, Kate reached out and stopped him. "Wait!" she said. She pointed to an area just beyond the next stairway. "There's the crab guy!"

8

I'll Catch That Pizza

"Wow! It sure looks like him!" Mike said. "Let's make like a crab and *pinch* him!"

The man with the bushy beard from the day before was standing behind a metal food stand just a little farther down the hallway. His baseball cap had a big white crab on it. A sign above the stand read OLD COVE CRAB SOUP.

A line of people was in front of the stand waiting for crab soup. The fans kept the man with the beard busy filling large paper cups with hot crab soup. The stand had a lower counter in front and large vats of crab soup on the left side. At the back of the stand was a small work area with a few boxes and other things on it.

"We need to find the glove," Kate said. "I bet he's got it hidden somewhere in the stand. He has to be able to take it out of the stadium without anyone seeing it."

"Let's sneak up behind the stand and snoop around," Mike said. "It looks like he's busy up front serving customers. I've got an idea."

Mike walked in the direction of the stand. But about halfway there, he moved over near the back wall. Then he squatted down and rocked back while extending his arms. He plopped his hands on the ground behind him and started to scuttle along the floor doing a crabwalk. "Come on," he said. "Let's pretend we're playing crab soccer!"

"Great idea!" Kate said.

Mike pulled his tennis ball out of his pocket and rolled it over to Kate as she dropped down near the wall and started to do a crabwalk, too. He and Kate scurried along the wall. Mike kicked the ball closer to the back of the crab stand, and then Kate kicked the ball. They continued until they were just behind the stand.

"There! We need to look at those!" Mike said. He pointed to a dark area behind the stand where there were stacks of large white buckets. "He could be hiding the glove in one of them!"

Mike grabbed his tennis ball and stood up. Kate shifted to her knees and reached for one of the white plastic buckets. Its white-and-blue label said OLD COVE CRAB SOUP. She popped the top off and looked inside. It was empty and smelled like crab soup. "Yum!" Kate said as

she put the cover back on and placed it to the side.

Mike did the same from the other side of the pile. They worked through the buckets one by one until they met in the middle.

"There's definitely no glove in those buckets," Mike said. "We need to look somewhere else." He surveyed the area. "The only other place he could be hiding the glove is in the stand," he said. "Here, I've got another idea. Let's play catch!"

Mike tossed the tennis ball to Kate, and she tossed it back to him. He took a few steps backward along the side of the stand while they continued to throw the ball back and forth. In between throws, they scanned the inside of the stand for possible hiding places.

The front of the stand held only the cash register, cups and spoons, and large pots of soup. At the back of the stand was a counter filled with newspapers, some plastic bags, a thermos, a bag of pretzels, and a pizza box.

Kate caught the ball and walked over to Mike. The line in front of the stand had gone down to one person. The man behind the counter had just handed the fan a cup of soup and taken her money. "Maybe it's under the newspapers," she said. "I'll keep him busy up front. You lean over the edge of the stand and check."

Mike nodded. "Okay," he said.

Kate headed for the front counter and waited for the other fan to finish. Mike slowly walked over to the back side of the stand. If the man turned around, he would clearly see Mike spying.

The customer in front took her change and walked away. Kate stepped up to the counter and winked at Mike.

"Can I please try samples of the different soups?" Kate asked.

As the soup man reached for plastic spoons to give Kate a taste, Mike darted to the side of the stand. He quietly ran his hands over the newspapers on the back counter and flattened them down. There was nothing under them.

The soup man offered Kate a second taste of soup.

Mike leaned farther over the wall of the stand and stuck his hand inside the pretzel bag. It struck something sharp and hard. He pulled out a pretzel stick. He stuck it in his mouth, and then motioned to Kate to keep going.

Mike leaned back over the low wall and grabbed for the pizza box, but his fingers just scraped the edge of the box. He pushed up on his tiptoes and slowly inched the box closer.

Mike checked the front of the stand. Kate was sampling more soup.

Mike pried the top of the pizza box up slightly. It was hard to see inside. He shifted the box and lifted the lid fully.

Inside the pizza box was an old, flat baseball glove!

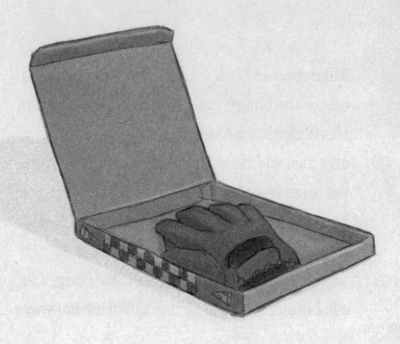

A Pitch Babe Ruth
Would Be Proud Of!

Mike reached back over the wall and grabbed one of the empty plastic bags on the counter. He checked to make sure it was clean and dry, and then slid Babe Ruth's baseball glove from the pizza box into the bag. He closed the pizza box, set it back down on the counter, and stepped away from the stand.

Kate was still tasting soup. Mike pointed to a hot dog cart a little farther down the hallway and motioned for her to meet him there.

A few moments later, Mike opened the plastic bag for Kate.

"You found the glove!" Kate whispered.

"Yes!" Mike said. "We've got to tell Flaps right away. I bet he'll pitch better knowing we've found the thief. Then we can turn it in to security and have them arrest the soup man."

Mike and Kate raced through the stadium and down the escalators to the lower level, where they ran to the aisle leading to the dugout. As they scrambled down the steps toward the field, a huge roar rose up from the Orioles fans. Many sprang to their feet to cheer and clap.

It was the bottom of the sixth inning. Flaps had gotten out of the last inning without giving up any more runs. And better yet, the Orioles had two runners on base and no outs. But they were still four runs behind Seattle.

All the clapping and cheering made it easy for Kate and Mike to jog to the very end of the aisle. It ran right next to the edge of the Orioles' dugout. Kate leaned over the small railing and waved her hands for attention. Finally, she caught the eye of an Orioles batboy and called him over.

"Please tell Flaps we found Babe Ruth's missing glove!" Kate said above the noise of the fans.

"Sure," the batboy said. He walked to the far side of the dugout, where Flaps was keeping his pitching arm warm in a jacket. The batboy whispered something in his ear.

Flaps looked over at Mike and Kate. He had a huge smile on his face and gave them a thumbs-up.

As the batboy was walking back, the fans exploded in cheers. The Orioles batter had hit a home run! Mike and Kate turned and watched as the ball sailed over the wall and landed in the Flag Court. The runners circled the bases and high-fived as they crossed home plate. With one hit, the Orioles had cut Seattle's lead to one run!

Kate felt a nudge on her arm. "Flaps says thanks!" the batboy said. "Because of you two, he's ready to get out there and shut Seattle down! He also said to meet him by the statue of Babe Ruth an hour after the game."

"Sure," Kate said. "Thanks for helping."

Mike and Kate stepped away from the dugout. The next Orioles batter walked up to the plate, and the fans settled back into their seats. "Come on," Kate said to Mike. "Let's turn the glove in and tell security about the soup man so they can arrest him."

"Okay," Mike said. "But then I want to head back to our seats to watch the game. Maybe Flaps will pitch just like Babe Ruth now!"

Catching Like the Babe!

Mike was right. For the rest of the game, Flaps pitched perfectly! He took out one batter after another, with strikeouts, pop-ups, and short hits to infielders. It looked like Seattle had lost its way. Or that Flaps had found his spot.

In between innings, Kate and Mike ran over to the barbecue stand. Mike bought a big pulled-pork sandwich, while Kate had a barbe-cue beef sandwich. As they munched on their food back at their seats, Mike pointed to the smoke from the barbecue stand.

"I don't know whether that's going east or west," he said. "But I think it's pointing to an Orioles win!"

In the top of the eighth inning, the Orioles knocked in one more run to tie the game. Seattle was hoping for a go-ahead run in the ninth, but Flaps shut them down by striking out the first three batters!

Now it was the Orioles' turn. The crowd roared to life as the Orioles batter stepped up to the plate. He watched two balls go by for strikes, but unloaded on the third. The ball flew high over the first baseman's head. It climbed higher and higher. The batter dropped the bat and started to run for first.

Then the stadium exploded in cheers as the

ball sailed over the wall. It was a walk-off home run! Flaps and the Orioles had won the game in the ninth inning! They had made it into the playoffs!

Mike and Kate cheered with the rest of the fans as the Orioles celebrated on the field. When Flaps came out and waved his hat at the crowd, the team quickly surrounded him and lifted him up for photos.

After the field cleared and fans started leaving, Mike and Kate met Kate's mom near the Kids' Corner, and they walked to the exit together as they told her what happened with the glove.

"There's the statue where we're supposed to meet Flaps!" Mike said. He pointed to a life-size statue of Babe Ruth just outside the main entrance to the Orioles' ballpark.

Kate studied the metal statue. It showed a

young Babe Ruth staring straight ahead, with a glove hanging from his right hand and a bat steadied against the ground in the other.

"It really looks like him," Kate said. She read the statue's title on the granite base. *"Babe's Dream.* I guess he's dreaming of winning a World Series."

"Or maybe he's dreaming of getting a left-handed fielder's glove!" Mike said. "Look at the glove he's holding. It's a right-handed fielder's glove. That means it's worn on the left hand. But Babe Ruth was a lefty! He would have had a *left-handed* fielder's glove, which is worn on his *right* hand! I can't believe they made such a huge mistake with this statue!"

"Good point, Mike," said a man's voice from behind them. "But he was a great pitcher, in any case!" Mike, Kate, and Mrs. Hopkins whirled around.

It was Flaps! He was still dressed in his uniform. Behind him was one of the Orioles clubhouse assistants carrying a cloth bag.

"You helped us make the playoffs!" he said. "I was so worried about the glove that I didn't pitch well until you found it!"

Flaps reached over and gave Mike and Kate dual fist bumps.

"The Old Cove Crab Soup man confessed after the police arrested him," Flaps said. "He told them he snuck into the stockroom just before lunch and stole the glove. He planned to sell it for lots of money. He left one of my gold coins in the hopes that the police would suspect me!"

Mike pointed to the glove on the statue. "At least we found the right glove," he said. "Or, should I say, the *left* glove!"

Flaps laughed. "Well, Mike," he said,

"you're right. They did make a mistake with this statue. Apparently, they gave the artist the wrong glove to use as a model, and when they found out it was wrong, it was too late to change it!"

Flaps turned to the clubhouse assistant.

"But it's not too late to share something with you," he said to Mike and Kate.

The assistant handed Flaps three pairs of white cotton gloves. Flaps gave Mike and Kate each a pair.

Mike pulled his gloves on. "Cool!" he said. "I can direct traffic now!" He made waving motions with his hands as though he were a policeman telling cars where to go.

"Mike, you might want to slow things down to get a look at this," Flaps said. He reached into the assistant's bag and pulled out something brown.

"How would you like to try on Babe Ruth's baseball glove?" Flaps asked. He held up the glove that Mike and Kate had rescued from the pizza stand.

"Wow-wee!" Kate said. "I'd love to!"

"Oh, cool!" Mike said.

"Since you and Mike found it, I thought you should both have a chance to try it on before it's put on display," Flaps said. "The white cotton gloves protect it from the oil on your hands. Go ahead, put it on!"

Kate gingerly slipped her hand into the glove. She tried to wiggle the fingers of the glove, but her hand wasn't quite big enough. She held up the glove and pretended to catch a ball. "This is great!" she said. "I feel like Babe Ruth! Thanks, Flaps."

She kept the glove on for a second, and then handed it over to Mike. He slipped it on carefully and felt the inside of the stiff, hundred-year-old glove.

"Hey, that reminds me," Mike said. "What did Babe Ruth's glove say to the baseball?"

Flaps shrugged. "I don't know," Kate said. "What?"

Mike held Babe Ruth's glove up like he was making a play. "Catch you later!"

Dugout Notes

☆ Baltimore Orioles ☆

Railroads and baseball. The proper name for the Orioles' ballpark is Oriole Park at Camden Yards. Originally, the Orioles played at Memorial Stadium in North Baltimore, which was also home to the Baltimore Colts football team. In 1992, the Orioles moved to a new ballpark in downtown Baltimore. Camden Yards was the name of the old railroad terminal where the new ballpark is located. The team wanted to call the new stadium Oriole Park, but the governor of Maryland wanted to call it Camden Yards. They compromised, and the ballpark was named Oriole Park at Camden Yards.

State birds and giant birds. The team is named after the state bird of Maryland, the Baltimore oriole. The team's mascot is a giant black-and-orange oriole. Its name is the Oriole Bird, but it's usually just called the Bird.

Lots of Orioles. Baltimore has had a number of baseball teams called the Orioles. Back in the early 1900s, there were two minor-league Baltimore teams called the Orioles at different times. Babe Ruth played on one of them.

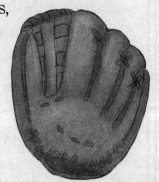

Today's Orioles moved from St. Louis (where they were the St. Louis Browns) after the 1953 season and changed their name to the Baltimore Orioles.

Babe Ruth and Baltimore. Babe Ruth only played baseball in Baltimore for about half a year before he was traded to the Boston Red Sox. His parents and grandparents lived in Baltimore, but Ruth lived at the St. Mary's Industrial School for Boys. His parents sent him to the school because Ruth got into too much trouble at home. He went there from age seven until he left to become a professional baseball player at age nineteen.

The mystery of Edgar Allan Poe. Edgar, the parrot in the story, is named after the great writer Edgar Allan Poe. He lived in Baltimore in the early 1830s, and he died mysteriously in Baltimore on October 7, 1849, after he was found outside, confused and in someone else's clothing. Poe is buried at the Westminster Hall and Burying Ground, near the ballpark. Poe is credited with inventing the detective story.

There's a street in the ballpark. Eutaw Street (pronounced Utah, like the state) is the street that runs along the giant B&O warehouse. But when the Orioles built their ballpark, they blocked off the area to traffic, so now it's part of the stadium and filled with fans during games. On non-game days, people can still walk down Eutaw Street and look in at the stadium through tall iron fences.

Eutaw Street home runs. If you walk down Eutaw Street, watch the ground! Sprinkled across the sidewalk are round bronze markers showing where really long home runs have landed. Usually a few new home runs land on Eutaw Street each year.

A national treasure. Baseball teams can thank Baltimore for the United States' national anthem. "The Star-Spangled Banner" was written in Baltimore by Francis Scott Key, who saw the American flag flying above Fort McHenry, in Baltimore Harbor, as the British bombed the fort in the War of 1812.

Statues and more statues. There really is a statue of Babe Ruth just outside the main gate of the stadium, with the wrong type of

glove. But the Orioles also have other statues inside the park. Orioles Legends Park has six large statues of famous Orioles: Frank Robinson, Brooks Robinson, Earl Weaver, Jim Palmer, Eddie Murray, and Cal Ripken Jr.

The Iron Man. One of the Orioles' most famous players was Cal Ripken Jr. Ripken's nickname was the Iron Man because he set the record for playing the most consecutive (which means "in a row") baseball games ever—2,632! As a shortstop and third baseman he was a nineteen-time All-Star and won two Gold Glove Awards. Many people think his record for most consecutive games will never be broken.

Pancakes for pitchers. While the character Flaps isn't real, Jim Palmer was a famous Orioles pitcher who always tried to have pancakes for breakfast on the days that he pitched, giving him the nickname Cakes. Palmer played his entire nineteen-year career for the Orioles and was elected to the Hall of Fame in 1990. When he was twenty, he pitched a complete-game shutout in the World Series!

The B&O warehouse. Behind the outfield and across Eutaw Street is the giant B&O warehouse. Railroads used to store goods there, but now it houses team offices, kitchens for the ballpark, restaurants, the Orioles' gift shop, and more. The 1,016-foot-long warehouse is the longest building on the East Coast, but it's also narrow, only fifty-one feet wide. So far only one batter has hit the building with a baseball. It was Ken Griffey Jr., the former Seattle Mariners outfielder, during a Home Run Derby in 1993. Make sure to look for a plaque on the warehouse that shows where he hit it. Nobody has broken a window yet.

A really long day. The Baltimore Orioles had a really bad day on August 22, 2007. That's because they lost a baseball game to the Texas Rangers by a score of 30–3! The Rangers scored the most runs in a major-league baseball game in 110 years!

Orange seats. The Orioles' stadium has two special orange seats in it that show where important home runs landed. One marks Eddie Murray's 500th home run.

The other marks where Cal Ripken's 278th home run landed. It broke the record (set by Ernie Banks) for home runs by a shortstop.

Flags a-flying. Overlooking the Orioles' right field is a large patio area filled with flag poles, called Flag Court. The flags represent the other American League teams and are flown in order of the divisional standings.

Crab Shuffle. During each game, the Orioles play Crab Shuffle on the giant video screen. One of three animated crabs grabs a baseball and hides it as the three crabs are shuffled around on the screen. Fans need to pick which crab is hiding the baseball!

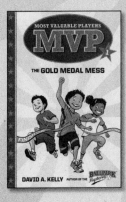
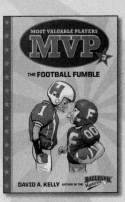

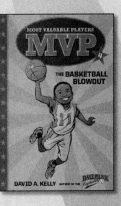

New friends. New adventures.
Find a new series . . . just for you!

ISADORA MOON

For ballerina and fairy and vampire lovers

COMMANDER IN CHEESE

For adventurers

JULIAN'S WORLD
THE STORIES JULIAN TELLS

For storytellers

PUPPY PIRATES

For dog lovers

PURRMAIDS

For mermaid and cat lovers

BALLPARK Mysteries

For sports fans

RHCB RHCBooks.com